For James MC-M

For my family and friends CC

First Edition
Published in Great Britain by ABC, All Books for Children,
a division of The All Children's Company Ltd.,
33 Museum Street, London WC1A 1LD, England
Library of Congress Cataloging-in-Publication Data
Conlon-McKenna, Marita.
    Little star / written by Marita Conlon-McKenna ; illustrated by Christopher Coady. – 1st ed.
        p. cm.
    Summary: After being added to a young boy's treasure collection,
a playful fallen star begins to dim, and the boy realizes that he must act to save her.
    ISBN 0-316-15375-3
    [1. Stars–Fiction.] I. Coady, Christopher, ill. II. Title.
PZ7.C761845Li   1993
[E]–dc20   92-22132
10 9 8 7 6 5 4 3 2 1
Published simultaneously in Canada by Little, Brown & Company (Canada) Limited
Printed in Hong Kong

Little Star

Written by
**MARITA
CONLON-MᶜKENNA**

Illustrated by
**CHRISTOPHER
COADY**

Little, Brown and Company
Boston Toronto London

The little star hovered over hot, sandy deserts and over snow-topped mountains. It sparkled over smoky city streets and gleamed over dark forests of green pines.

It winked at the waves and smiled for the animals in the jungles.

Then, one night, the star fell and fell until it landed, in the middle of a patch of weeds at the back of a garden.

"James! It's getting dark. Time to come in!"

James stopped. There were dark shadows everywhere. He dodged and ran through them with his ball.

Near the flower bed, something caught his eye. The little star twinkled. It twinkled at James. He bent down to see what it was. "Whatever it is, it's glowing," James whispered.

He touched it. It was warm, almost hot. He picked it up, and it stung his fingers. "Ouch!" James almost dropped it. He held it in one hand and touched it with the other. It felt rough and sharp. He turned it over and then on its side, but he couldn't figure out what it was.

"James!"

"Coming!"

James hid the sparkling shape inside his jacket, raced
up to his room, and put it with his collection of treasures.
Soon it was time for his good-night story. James closed his eyes.
Then Mom went downstairs, clicking off the light as she left.

James sat up in bed. He had been asleep.
"It must be the middle of the night," he thought.
He could hear the clock ticking on the landing.
His light was off, but the bright glow coming
from his shelf lit up the entire room. James
got up and went to look.

His shape was winking and twinkling.
"Oh!" he cried. "You're a star!"

Suddenly, the star flew across the room. She z . . . z . . . zinged from place to place. She swooped and dived and spun and really showed off.

Then the room grew dim. When James's eyes got used to the dark, he looked for her.

She was hiding under his bed!

"Star!" he called. She jumped out, then disappeared again. James found her in his toy box.

"So that's it," laughed James. "Hide-and-seek!" They played until James grew tired and went back to bed.

The next morning, James whispered, "Hello," but when he touched her, she felt cooler, and hard.

James could hardly wait for night to come. And again, the star shone and twirled around the room. But this time she didn't want to hide. James thought she was looking for something.

"Do you want to see my toys?" he asked her. He emptied his toy box. All his cars lay spread out on the carpet.

But the star seemed bored. Suddenly, James thought of something. "This is my farm set! It's my very best toy!"

One by one, he lifted up the animals and showed them
to the star: the cow, the big horses, and the fat pig.
She seemed to recognize them and lit each one in turn.
James yawned. "I'll clean up in the morning," he said.
The star watched over them all as James slept.

By the third night, the light from the star wasn't as bright.
She glided slowly around the room and stopped in front of the window.
    James was tired and stayed in bed. "Would you like to see my books?"
he asked. "This is about a boy called Jack who climbed up a giant
beanstalk." As he turned the pages, the star rested on his pillow.
Her light dimmed, like a flashlight growing old. His skin no longer
felt hot when she was near. His eyes closed.
    The book slipped from his hands, and he was asleep.

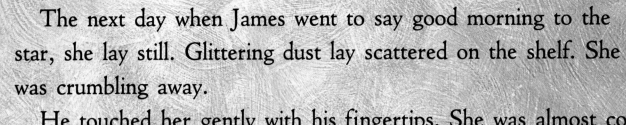

The next day when James went to say good morning to the star, she lay still. Glittering dust lay scattered on the shelf. She was crumbling away.

He touched her gently with his fingertips. She was almost cold and felt brittle and rough.

His star was dying!

Soon there would be nothing left but shiny dust.

"Oh, star!" he whispered to her.

That night, he put the star in his jacket and carried her outside to the backyard. All around was darkness. He looked at her one last time.

"Good-bye, little star," he whispered.

Then, with one huge stretch, he *flung* the star as far as he could into the blackness. Then he turned and raced inside without looking back.

That night his bedroom seemed lonely, and his
treasure shelf looked dull. Mom came to tuck him in.
"You don't even need the light tonight," she said,
"it's so bright from the stars."
James pressed his hand against the window.
High above, the little star flashed
and danced and twinkled
. . . just for James.